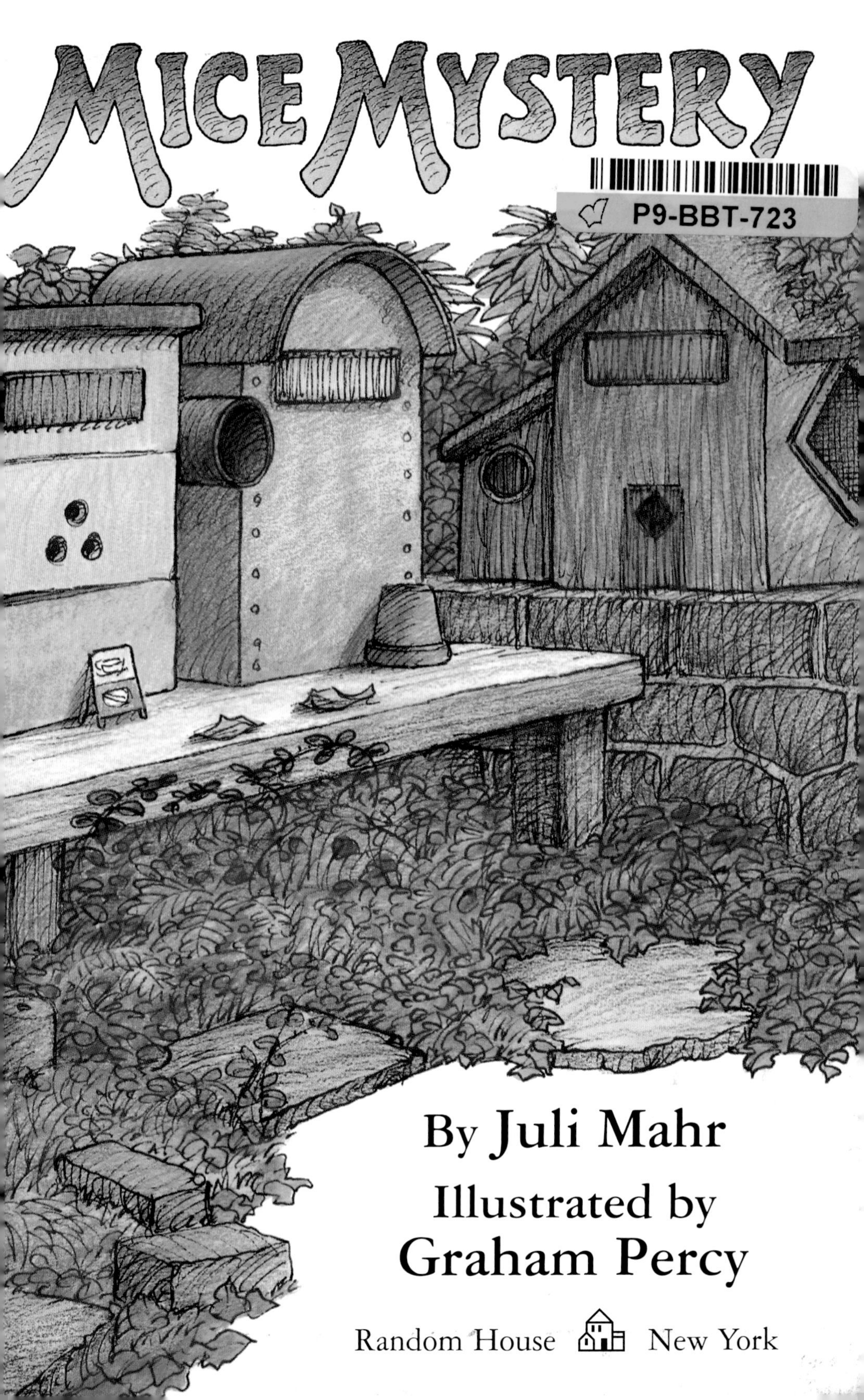

MICE MYSTERY

By Juli Mahr
Illustrated by
Graham Percy

Random House New York

Watson Mouse lived in the first mailbox on Ivy Row, Little Falls. Although he worked in the mayor's office, Watson dreamed of being a great detective. In fact, he talked of little else.

One morning the special package that Watson had been waiting for finally arrived. He couldn't wait to open it!

TO: Mr. W. Mouse
Wannabe Detective
Ivy Row
Little Falls
Mouseachusetts

URGENT

Watson crawled back into bed to read his new manual from cover to cover. Finally he could be a famous detective! Now all he needed was a case to solve.

Watson was so excited that he almost forgot to go to work. He put on his hat, brushed his whiskers, and raced into the kitchen to make breakfast.

"That's strange," he thought. "I'm sure the fridge was full of cheese yesterday. I guess I'll have to pick up something at Luigi's."

But even Luigi was out of cheese.

"Stranger and stranger," thought Watson. Something fishy was going on, but he couldn't quite put his paw on what.

Just then a speeding car screeched around the corner and almost knocked him over.

"Hmm," grumbled Watson, "that's Cousin Louis. What's *he* doing in town?"

By the time Watson arrived at the office, he was very hungry. Thank goodness he was going to his mom's for lunch.

A flowery letter was waiting for him on his desk. "Hmm, I wonder who this is from?" said Watson.

To Watson Mouse
The most talented, intelligent,
and handsome mouse
in the world.
At the Mayor's Office
Stamp-Licking Department
Town Hall

Wuffy,
Special
Hand Delivery

"Wait a minute!" thought Watson as his nose began to twitch (a sure sign that trouble was coming). "What's happened to all the cheese?"

Watson needed to think things over. At noon he headed for Miss Whiskers's Luncheonette . . . if anyone had some cheese, she would.

But Watson found Miss Whiskers in despair. "Somebody's taken all the cheese . . . every last chunk of it. What's happening in this crazy town?" she cried.

Watson's nose began to twitch again. This was a serious crime. Perhaps the biggest Little Falls had ever seen!

"Don't worry, Miss Whiskers," said Watson eagerly. "I know just what to do."

Rule One
SEARCH FOR CLUES

Watson followed Marlowe Mouse's instructions from *How to Be a Famous Detective*.

He wiggled his ears to hear things . . .

twitched his nose to smell things . . .

and used his magnifying glass to look for clues.

Nothing here . . .

Nope, nothing at all.

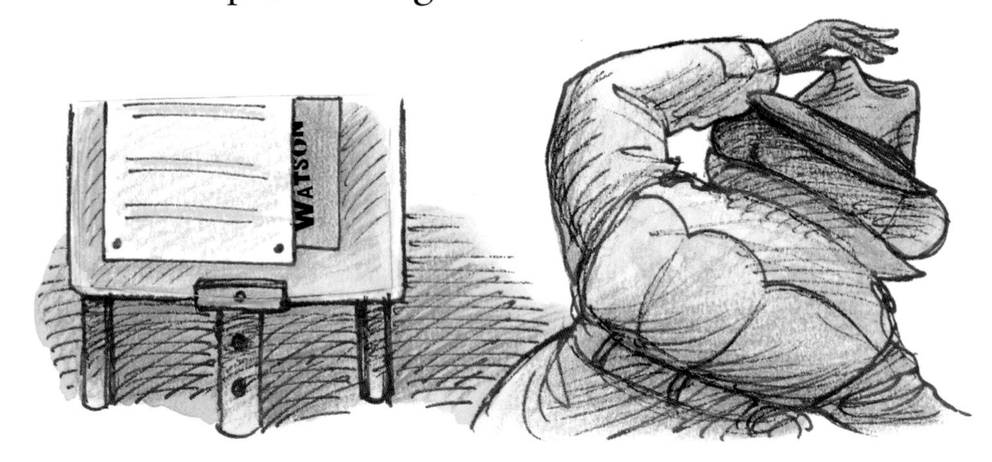

"Watson," said Miss Whiskers finally. "What's this envelope stuck on my menu board?"

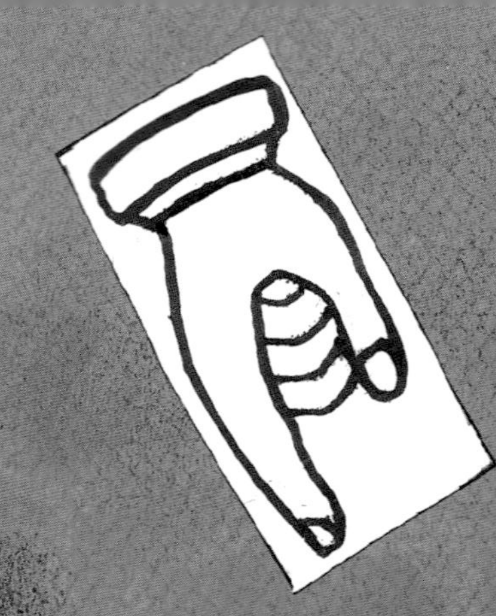

WATSON

SON-T

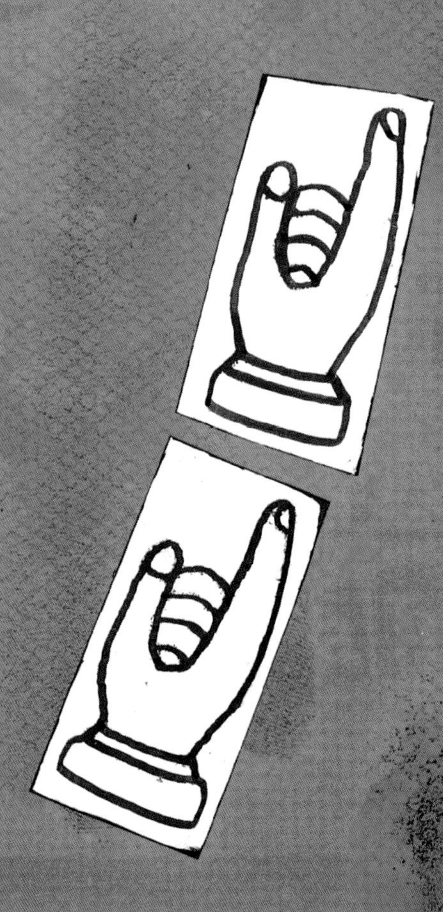

As Watson read the warning note, Miss Whiskers squeaked, “Look, Watson, paw prints!”

Watson stared blankly at the oily tracks.

“They could be from the thief,” she hinted. “A thief with just two toes.”

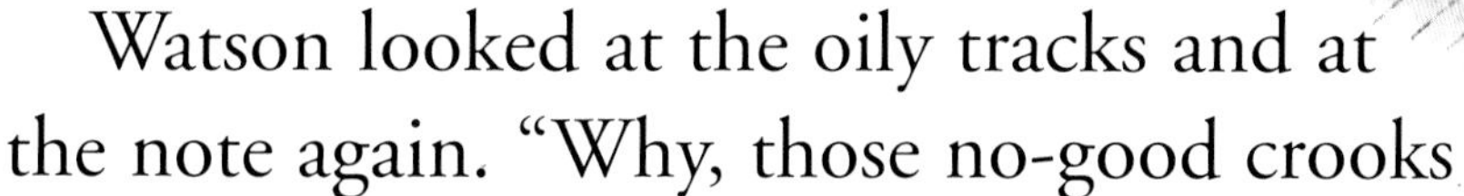

Watson looked at the oily tracks and at the note again. “Why, those no-good crooks . . . they can’t keep *me* off their trail!”

Rule Two
FOLLOW ANY CLUES

So Watson followed the paw prints. He crawled out of the luncheonette,

down the street,

and past the school bus stop.

At the end of the trail he found another envelope.

To Sir Watson

ou hast not a chance.
thee up the chase
il leads nowh
lost ca

Rule Three

IF THE TRAIL RUNS COLD, GO BACK TO THE SCENE OF THE CRIME

Robbers always do

"Me? Give up? Never!" Watson said.

He returned to Miss Whiskers's Luncheonette and waited in disguise.

He'd catch the thieves, even if he had to wait

. . . and wait

. . . and wait.

Finally Watson was rewarded when an envelope landed on his nose.

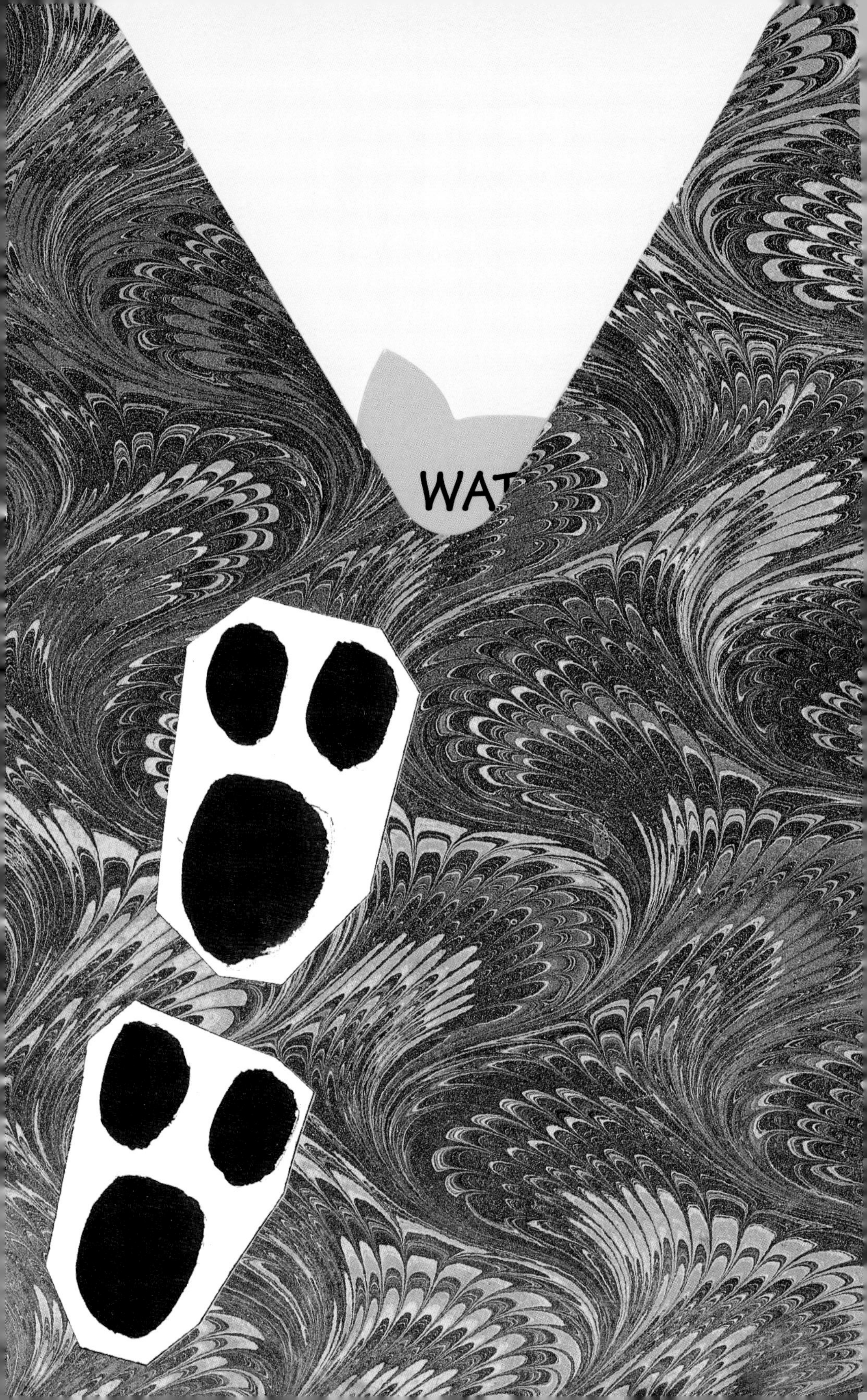
WAT

Watson raced into the luncheonette. "I think I've found something, Miss Whiskers!" he said excitedly. "If only I could read this foreign language."

Miss Whiskers looked in her mirror to check her lipstick. "Why don't you use my mirror, Watson?"

Watson took a long look at himself in her mirror.

“No, Watson. Use the mirror to *read* the note!” Miss Whiskers sighed.

“A cat? But cats have four toes and those prints had only two,” Watson said. “Wait a minute . . . ” His nose began to twitch double time.

Rule Four
DO YOUR HOMEWORK

Watson scurried over to the police station. Only he wasn't going there to report the crime. He was going there to look at *The Big Book of Most-Wanted Cats*. If his hunch was right . . .

Rule Five

WHEN YOU ARE CLOSE TO SOLVING THE CRIME— WAIT AND WATCH

Watson set out for the garbage dump where Two-Toes Jackson lived. He searched among the trash, but he had no luck. Just as he was about to leave, he spotted the shadows of two cats behind some laundry. He crept up close to listen.

“Okay, Two-Toes,” said a cat with a strange, loud voice. “This is what we do: we send another note to put Watson off our trail. Then I’ll take the cheese back to the city. You sure it’s safe where we hid it?”

“Don’t worry, boss. He’ll never find it,” meowed Two-Toes.

“I hid the cheese in the last place he’d ever look—his office!” snickered Two-Toes.

“Why, those no-good cats!” thought Watson, and he scrambled through the garbage and raced to his office. “I’ll show them! I’ll save the cheese!”

But just as he was passing Luigi's cheese stand, a car screeched around the corner and almost knocked him over. Cousin Louis again! After Watson saved the cheese, he really would have to find out what Cousin Louis was doing in Little Falls.

At his office Watson heard a loud squeak for help. It was Miss Whiskers! No time to waste! With his knees trembling and his whiskers shaking, Watson opened the door.

“Happy birthday!” shouted Miss Whiskers, Watson’s mother, and all of his friends—even Cousin Louis. Silly Watson, he’d forgotten that it was his birthday! So *that’s* where all the cheese had gone—into the biggest birthday party ever, with cheese cake, cheese pies, and cheese shakes.

RPRISE
PROUD
MOM

"Ladies and gentlemice," said the mayor after Watson had blown out the candles. "I think you'll agree that Watson Mouse deserves to be a Little Falls detective! From now on, if there's a mystery, you know who can solve it!"